Sound at Sight

2nd series

Sight reading for Piano

Book 1

Initial–Grade 2

Published by:
Trinity College London
www.trinitycollege.com

Registered in England
Company no. 02683033
Charity no. 1014792

Third impression, October 2014

Printed in England by the Halstan Printing Group, Amersham, Bucks.

Sound at Sight 2nd series

Playing or singing music that has not been seen before is a necessary part of any musician's life, and the exploration of a new piece should be an enjoyable and stimulating process.

Reading music requires two main things: first, the ability to grasp the meaning of music notation on the page, and second, the ability to convert sight into sound and perform the piece. This involves imagining the sound of the music before playing it. This in turn implies familiarity with intervals, chord shapes, rhythmic patterns and textures. The material in this series will help pianists to develop their skills and increase confidence.

This second series of *Sound at Sight* builds on the first, by adding a plethora of new exercises for each level. These newly composed pieces have been written by a variety of leading educational composers in a wide range of styles, realistically reflecting what students will encounter in their progressive study of the instrument. This in turn provides essential exam preparation.

Trinity's sight reading requirements are stepped progressively between Initial and Grade 8, with manageable increases in difficulty between each grade. Exercises at Initial to Grade 2 have been given descriptive titles in order to help stimulate the imagination. Towards the end of each grade selection in this book, some exercises may be a little more challenging than the exam criteria, but attempts at these will ensure that candidates are amply prepared. Some tips on exam preparation are given at the back of this book, along with an at-a-glance table of the requirements at each level.

Contents

Trinity College London would like to thank Mike Cornick, Robin Hagues, Robert Ramskill and John York for their work on this series.

Initial

Music will always be at **Moderato** tempo in C major, with the notes laid out in a 5-finger position. Dynamics will always be ***f*** and ***p***, and the time signature $\frac{2}{4}$.

1 Fanfare

2 Parachute Jump

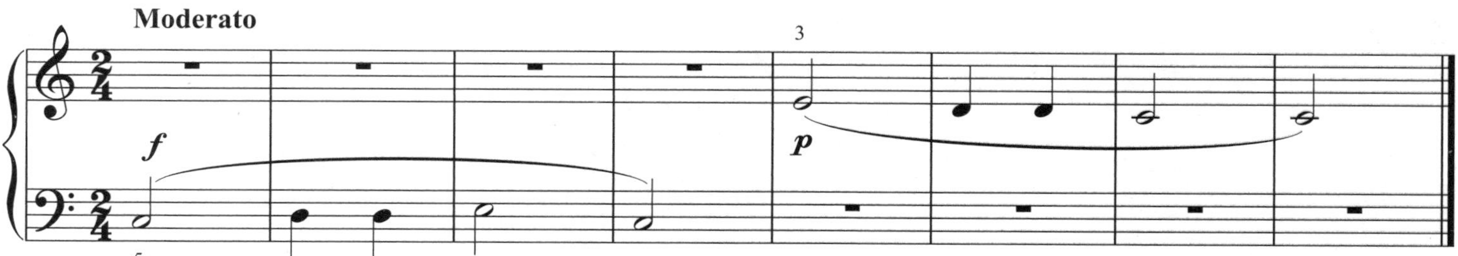

3 Up and Down

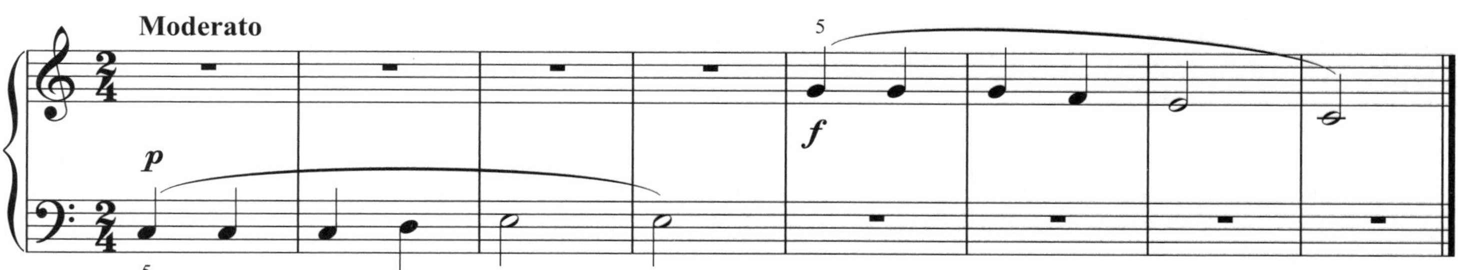

4 Summer and Autumn

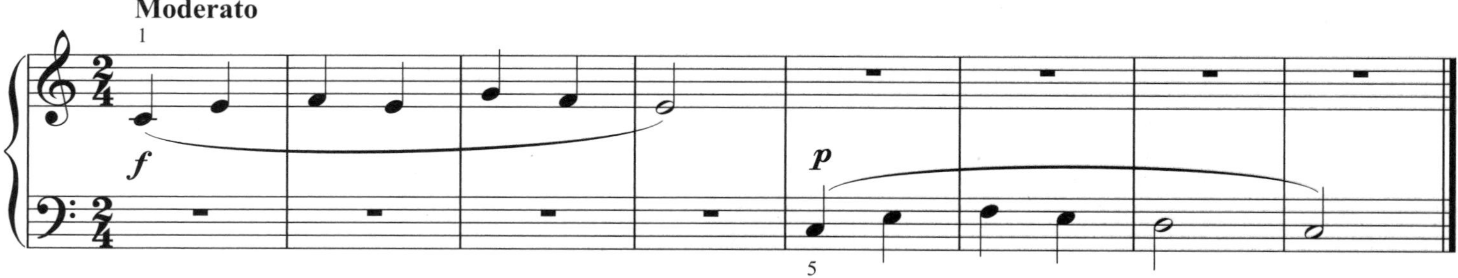

5 Question and Answer

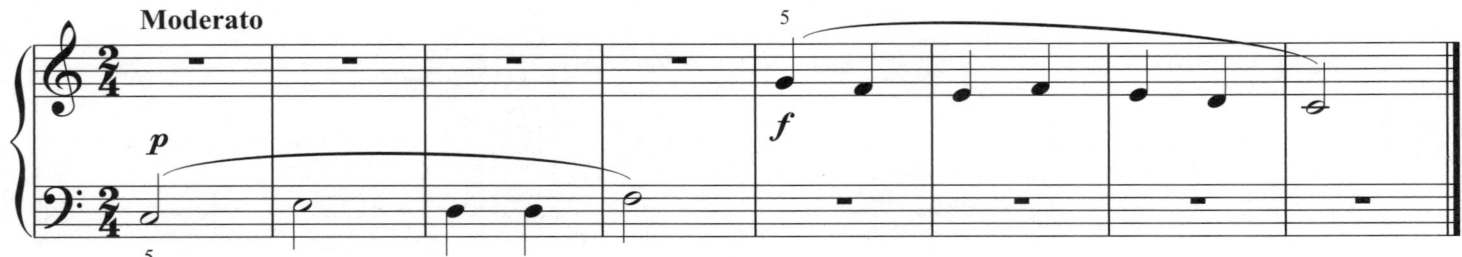

6 Stepping Stones

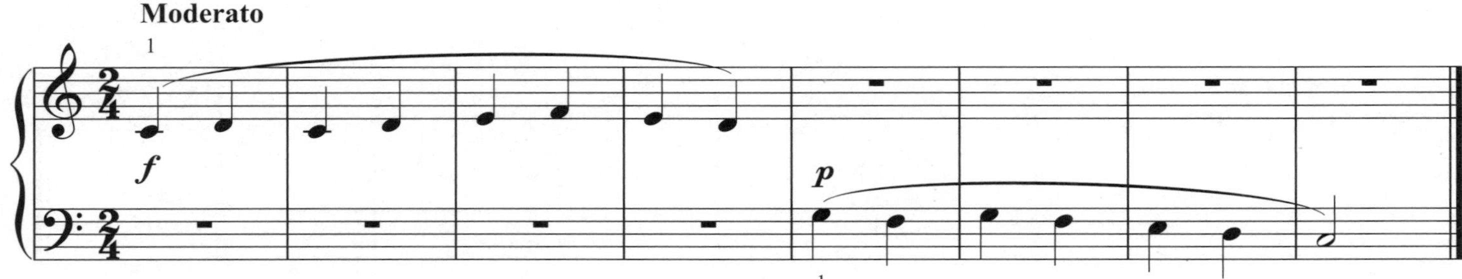

7 Copy Cat

8 Rocking

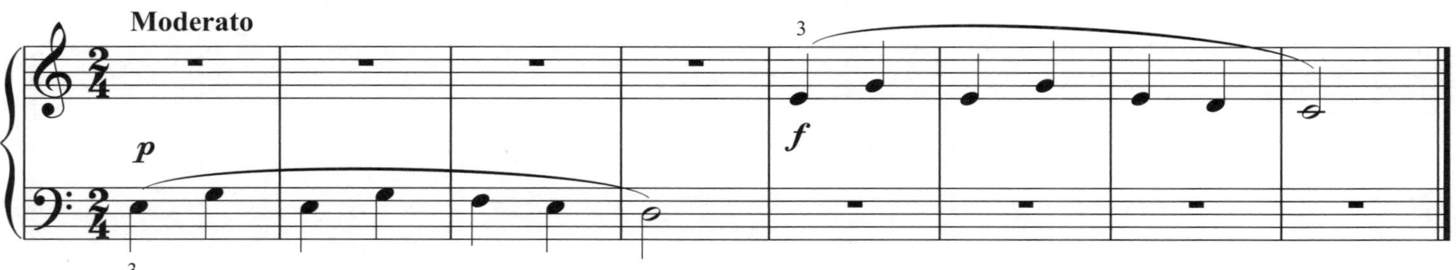

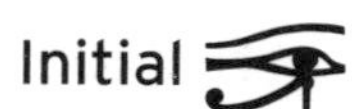

9 Conversation

10 March

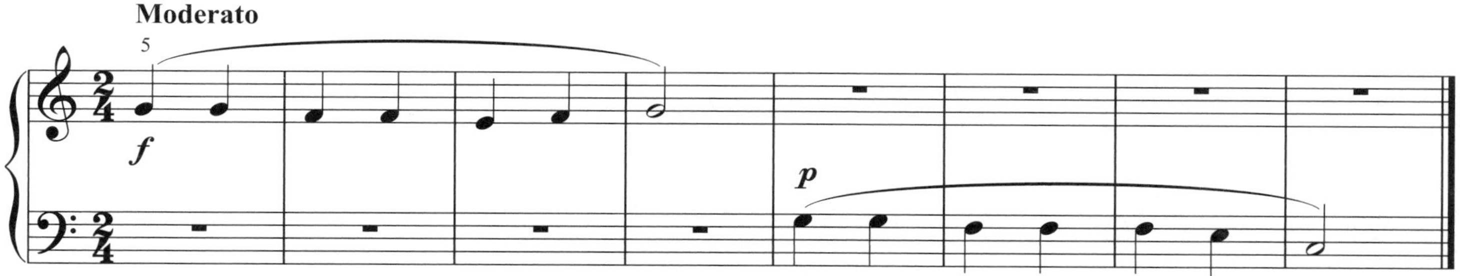

11 Ready To Go

12 Follow Me

13 In the Morning

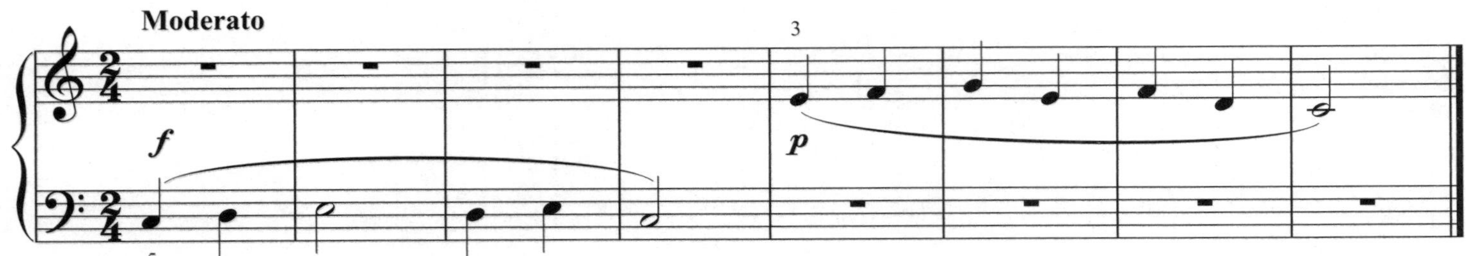

14 Drifting Asleep

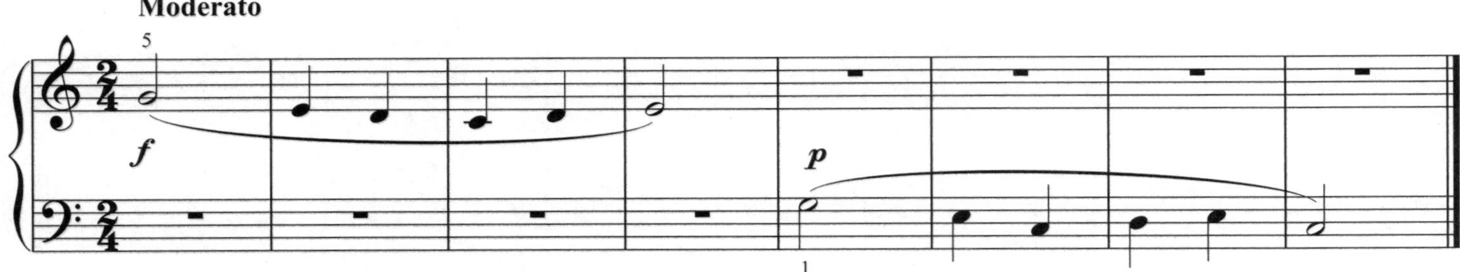

15 Tea and Coffee

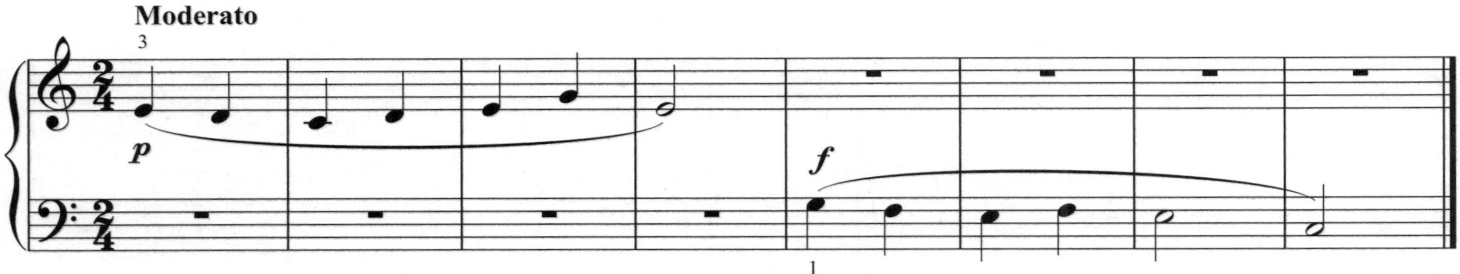

16 Waking Up

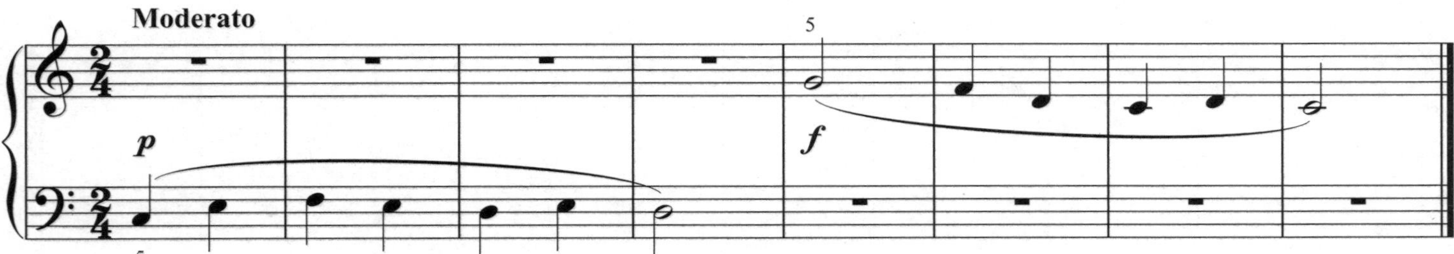

17 Winter and Spring

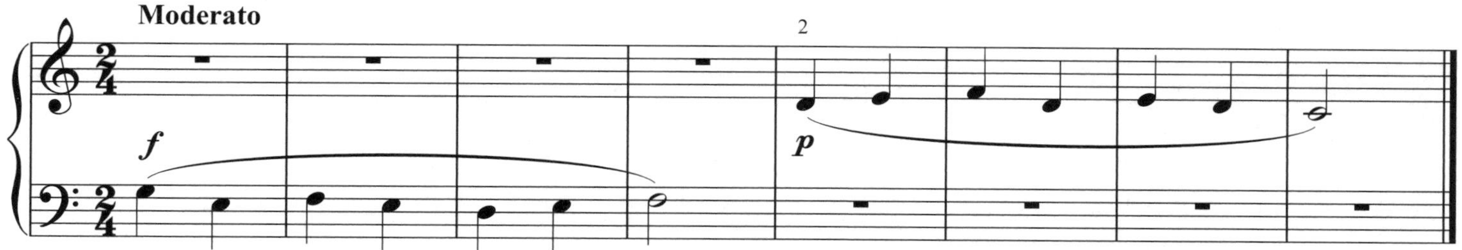

18 Snowflakes

19 Leaping Lambs

20 Stretching

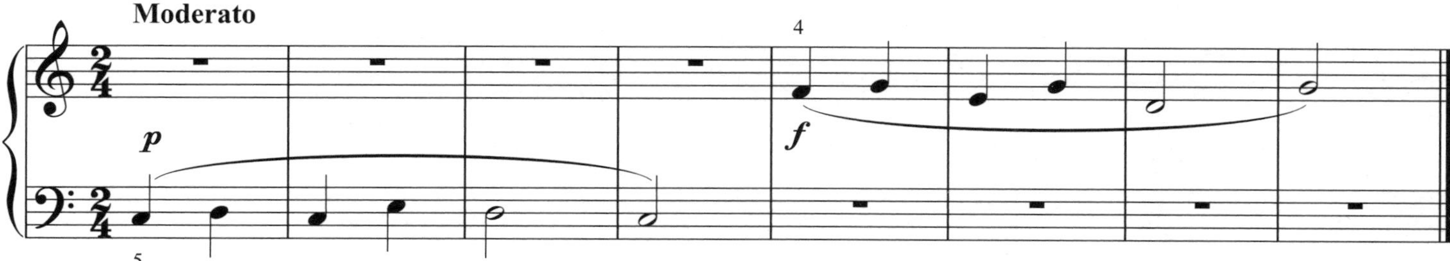

21 Bugle Call

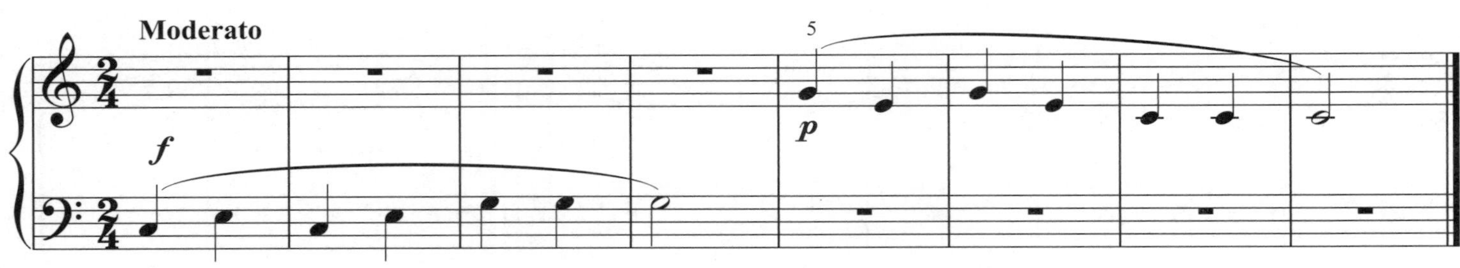

22 Floating

23 Waves

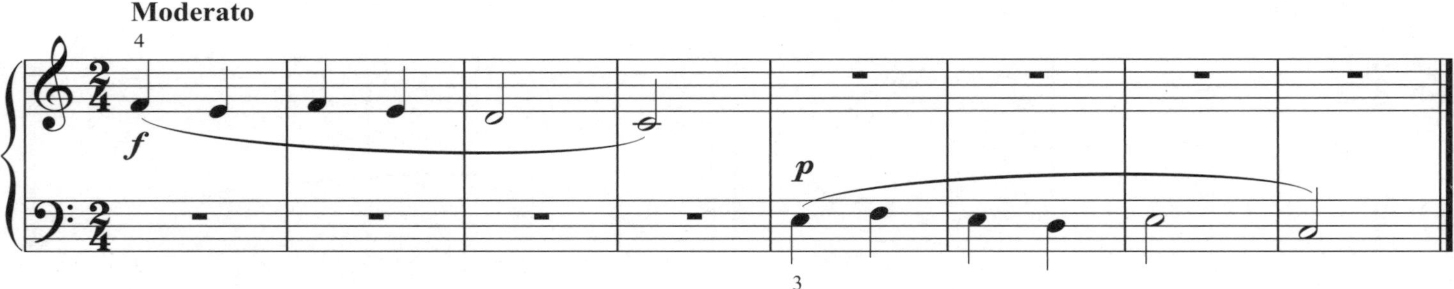

24 Mirror

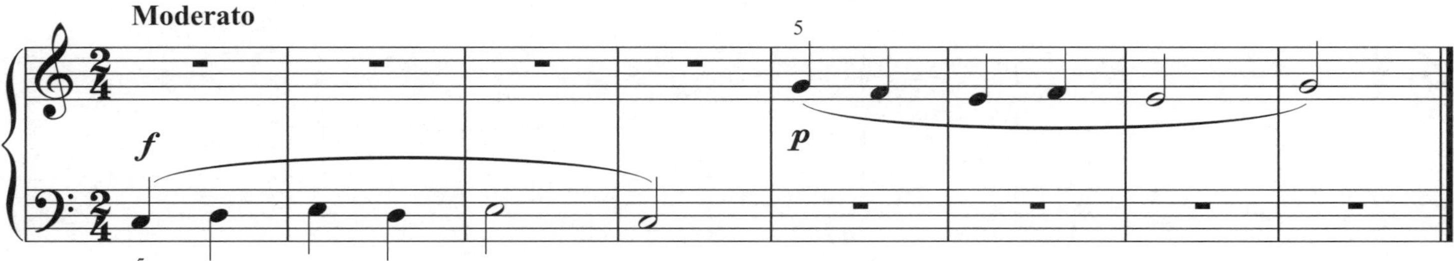

25 A Brave Start

26 Lost and Found

27 On the Stairs

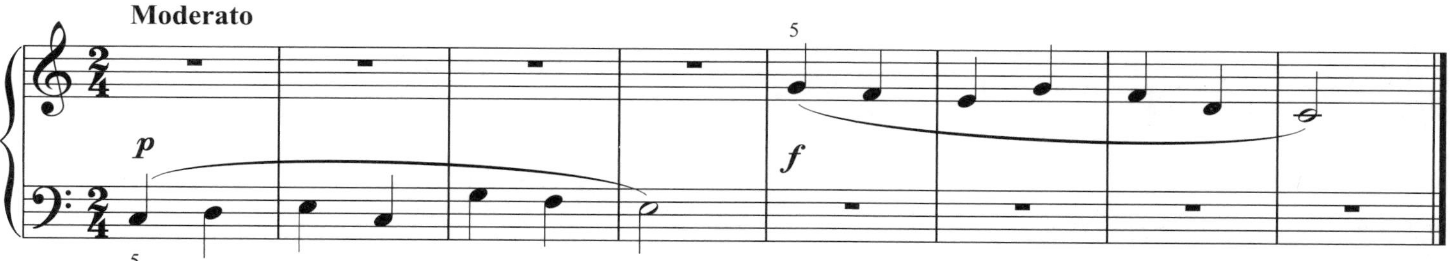

28 Tip-toe Away

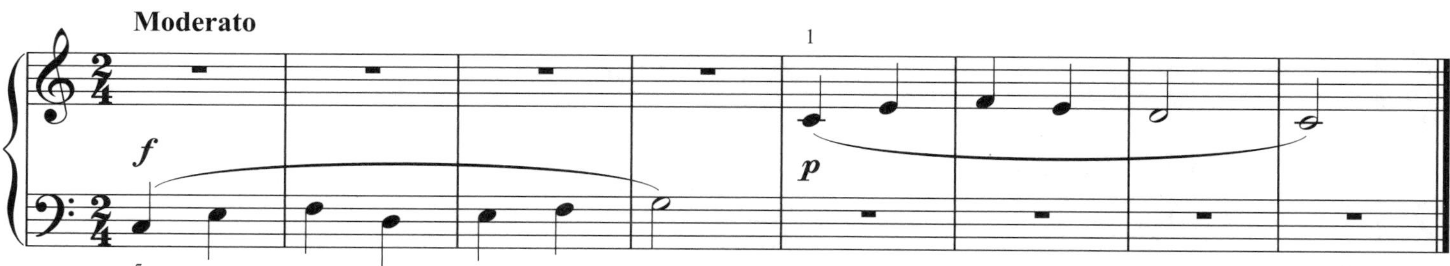

Grade 1

The keys of G major and A minor (white notes only) are added at this level, as well as semibreve notes and 4/4 time. ***mf*** is added, and hands may also play simple music together.

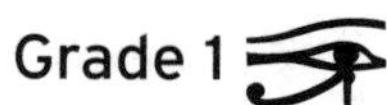

5 Robot March

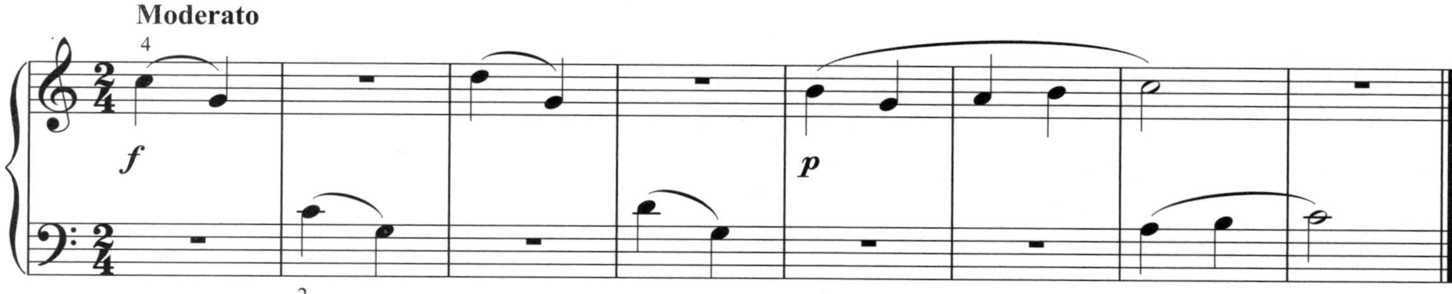

6 Lonely

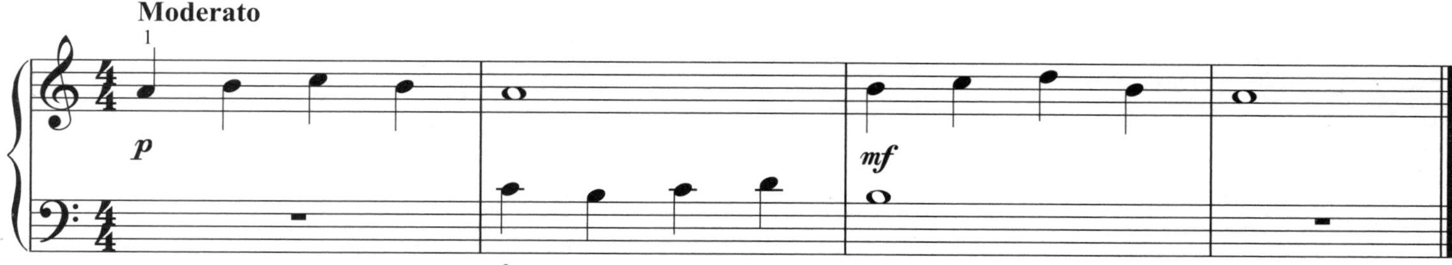

7 Riding

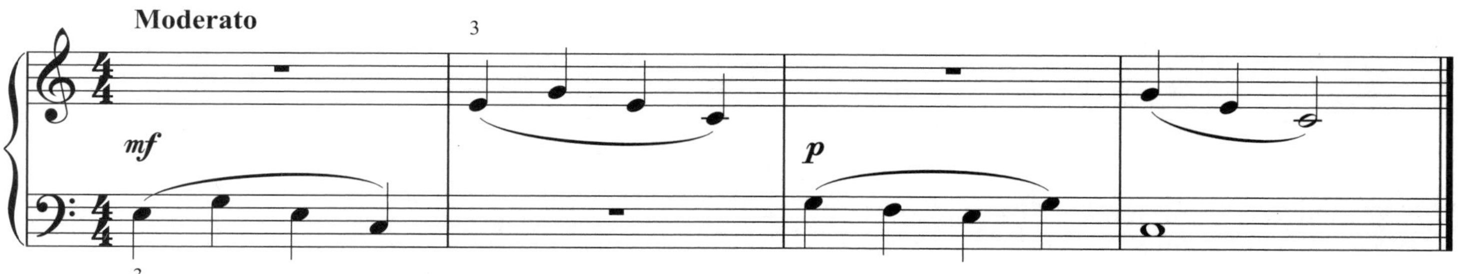

8 Positive Thinking

9 Floating

10 Summer Rain

11 Little Dance

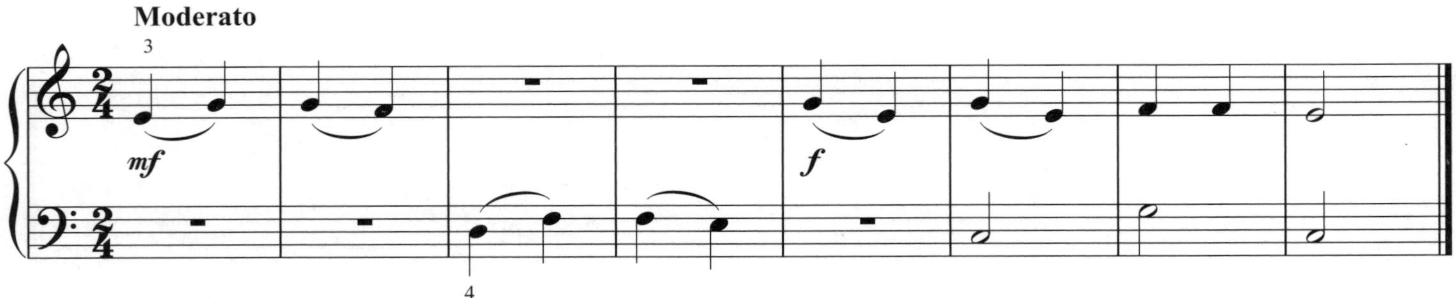

12 Pointing

13 Zero Gravity

14 Small Steps

15 A Short Story

16 A Minor March

17 A Day Out

18 Strolling

19 Cat Walk

20 Jumping

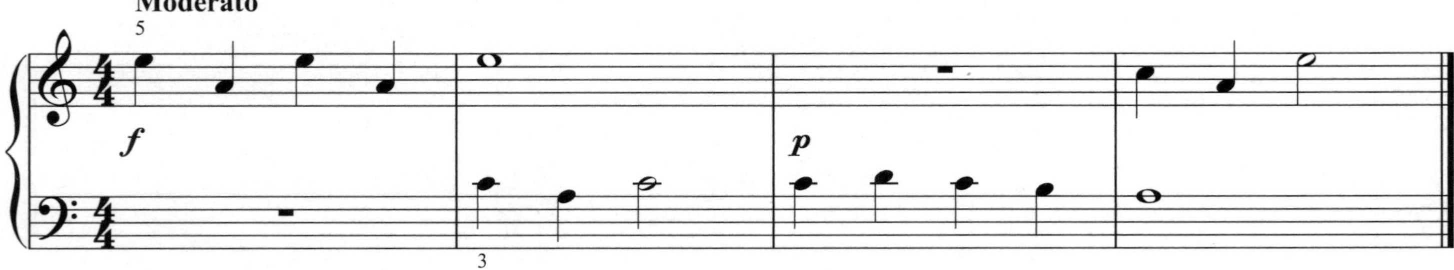

21 Musical Moment

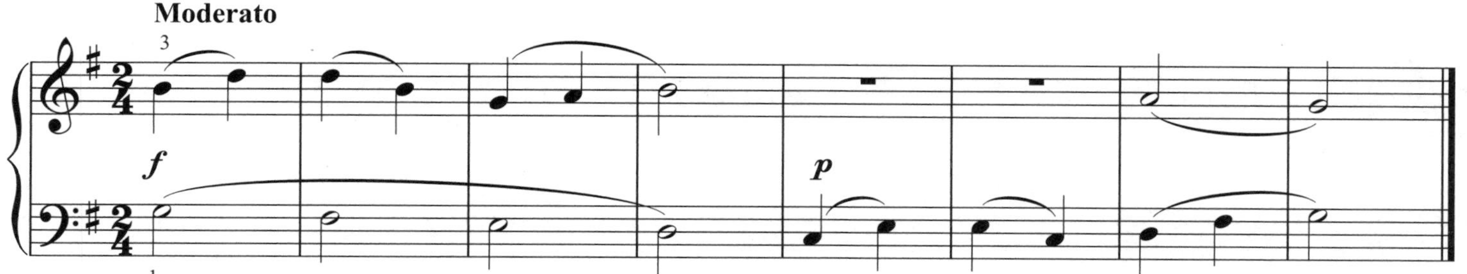

22 Clock

23 Tortoise

24 Thought for the Day

25 Tunelet

26 Piggy-back

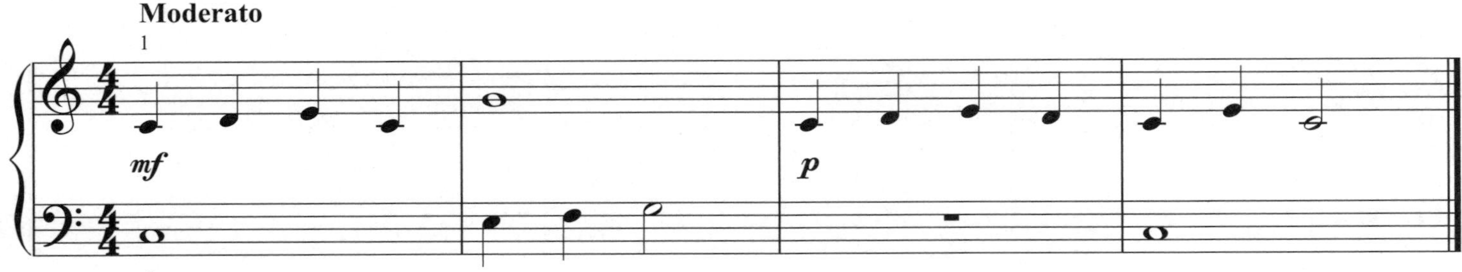

27 Mood Change

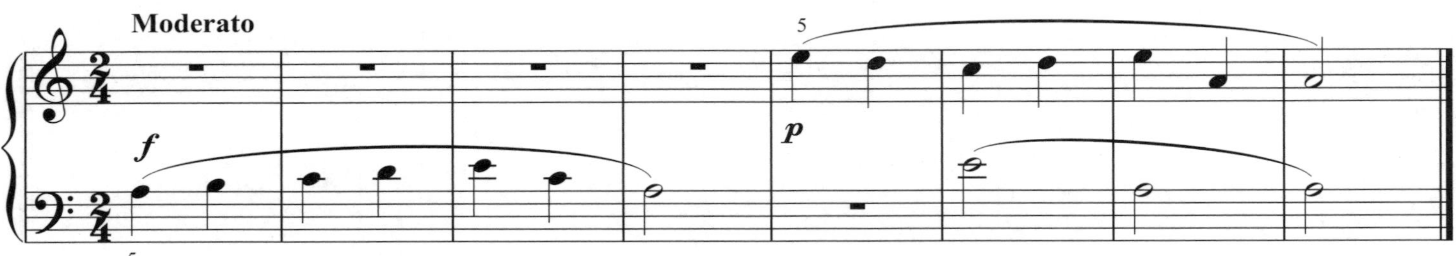

28 Calm Reply

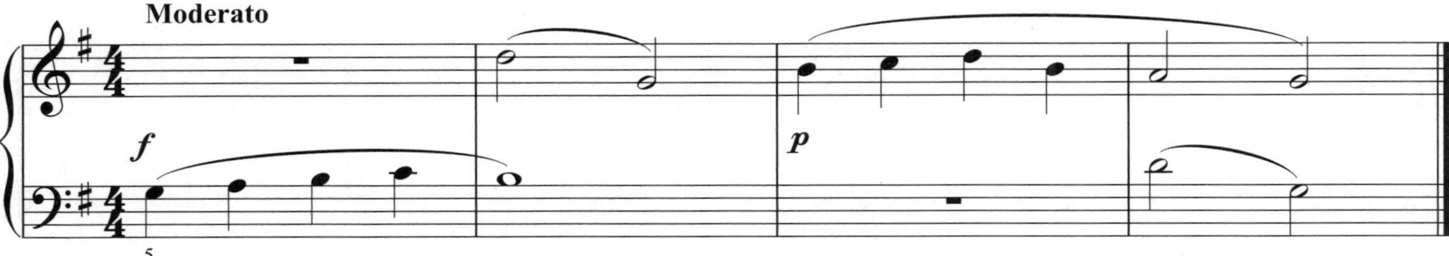

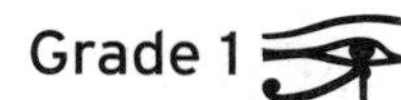

29 No Worries

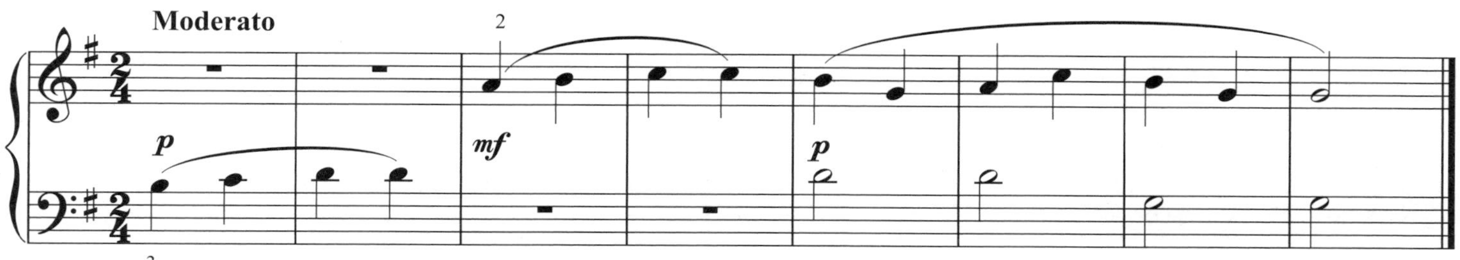

30 Brief Encounter

31 Chaser

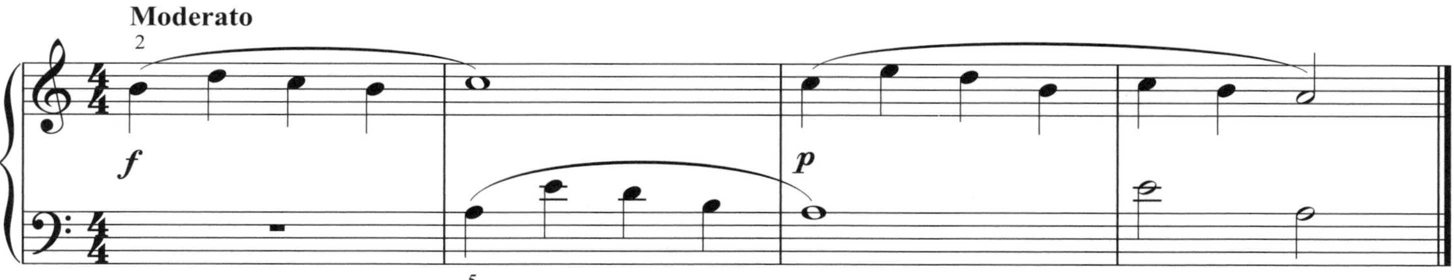

32 Ski Slope

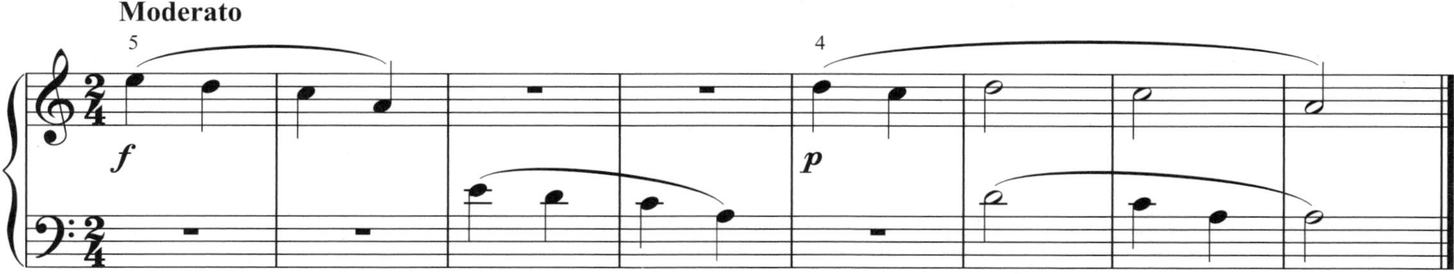

Grade 2

G♯ is included within A minor at this level, along with $\frac{3}{4}$ time. Tempi can also include **Allegretto** and dotted minims, and tied notes may be used. More consistent two-part textures are now involved.

1 Finger and Thumb

2 Woodland Walk

3 Sharp-shooting

4 Close-up

5 Jumping Up

6 Peas and Carrots

7 One Two Three

8 Lament

9 Island Hopping

10 Echoes

11 Lions at the Watering Hole

12 Tandem Ride

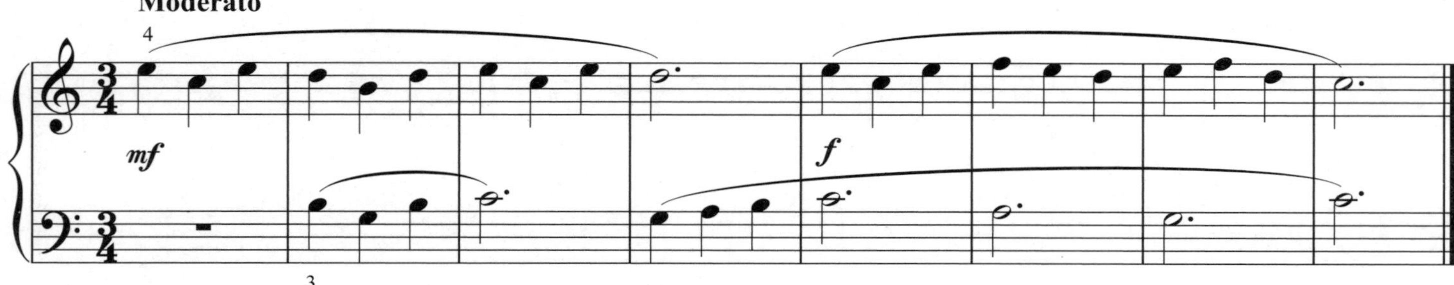

13 Clouds

14 Snake Charmer

15 Sunny Day Walkabout

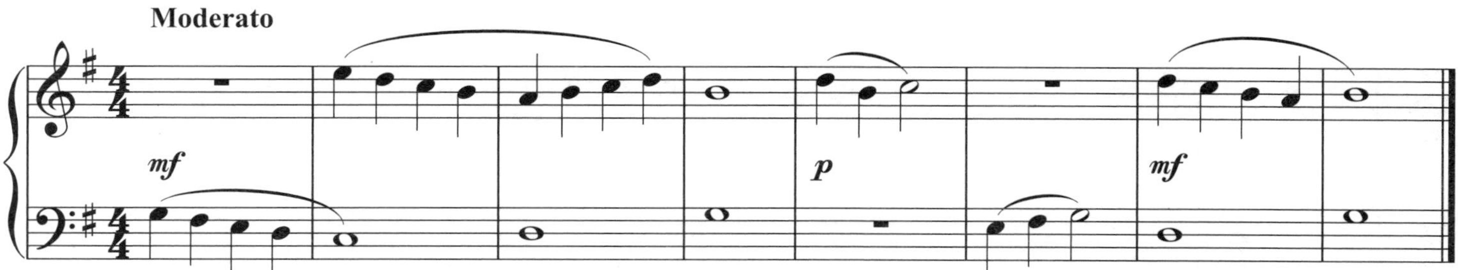

16 High Fives

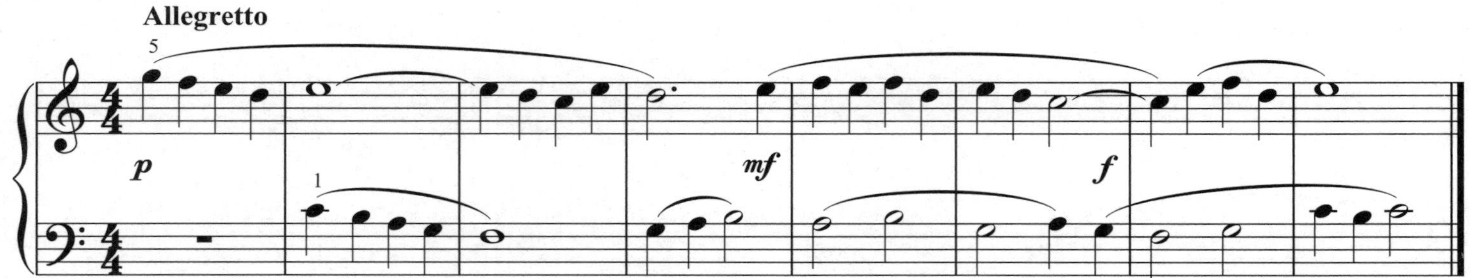

17 Once upon a time ...

18 Spring

19 Minuet

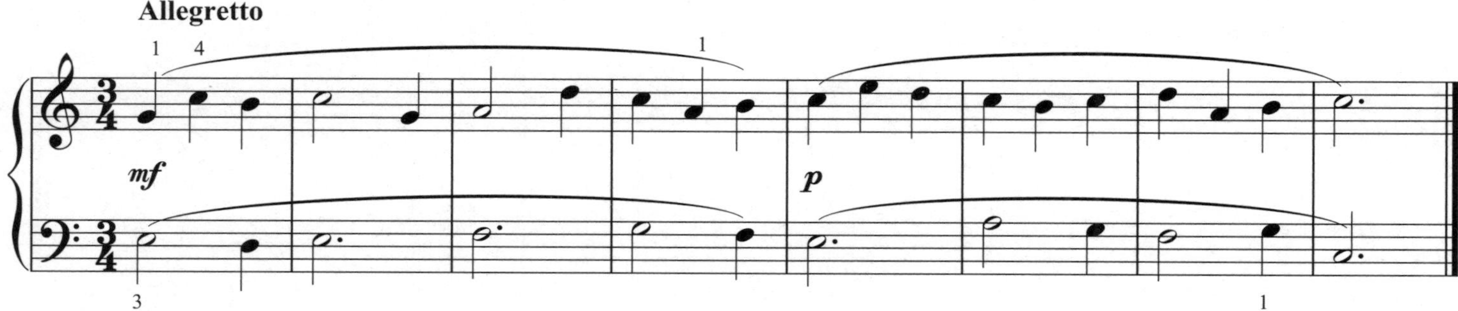

20 Daydream

21 Tadpoles

22 Jogging

23 Dance!

24 Poplars

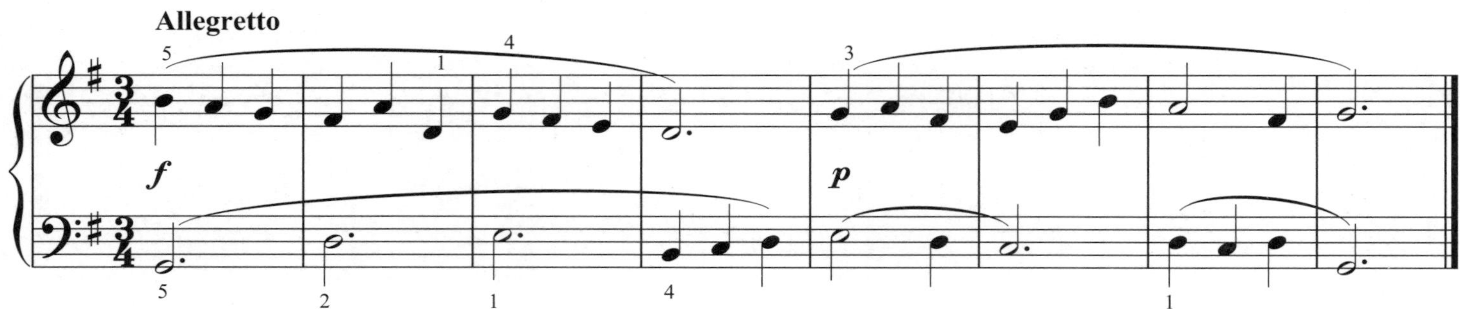

25 Walking Away

26 Reflection

27 Whooshing Reeds

28 Afternoon Tea

29 Splashing in Puddles

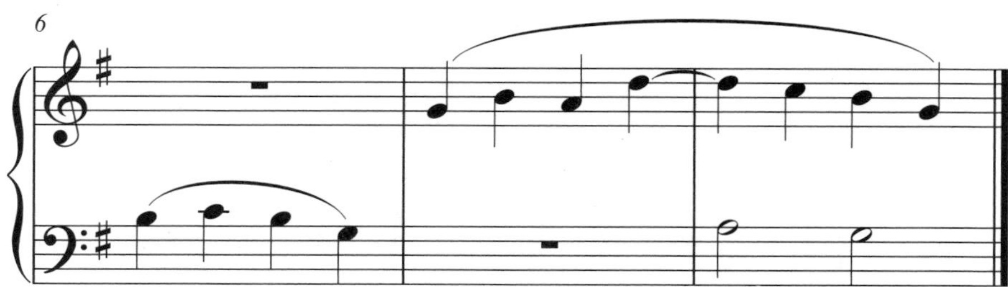

30 Thinking Time

31 Never Stop

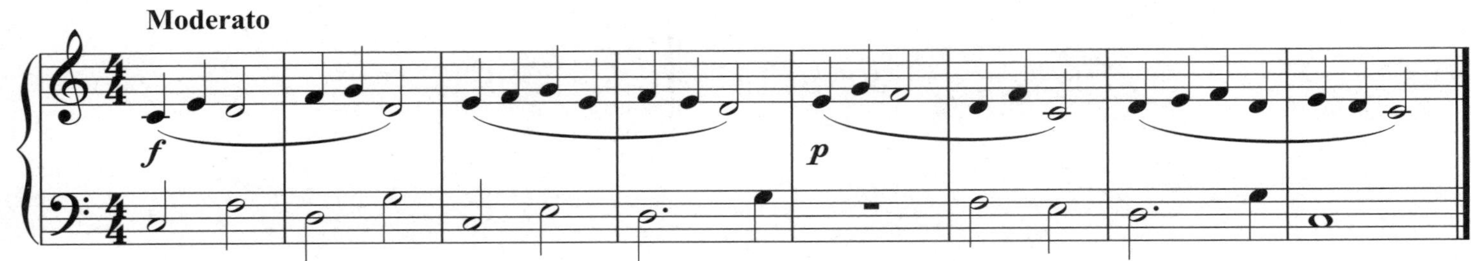

32 The Show Goes On

33 Running Smoothly

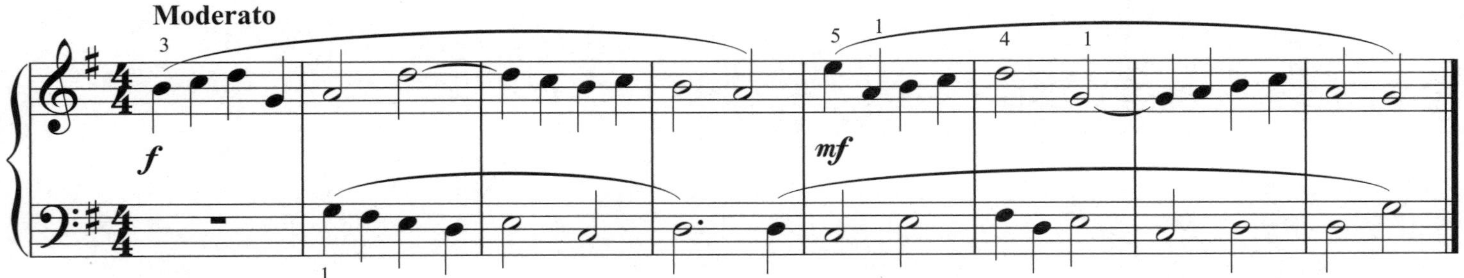

34 Valsette

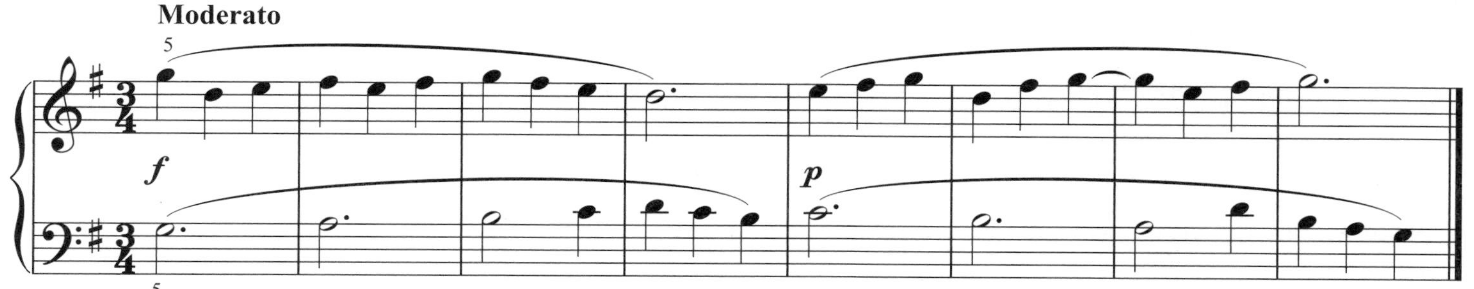

35 Red Alert

36 Looking Back

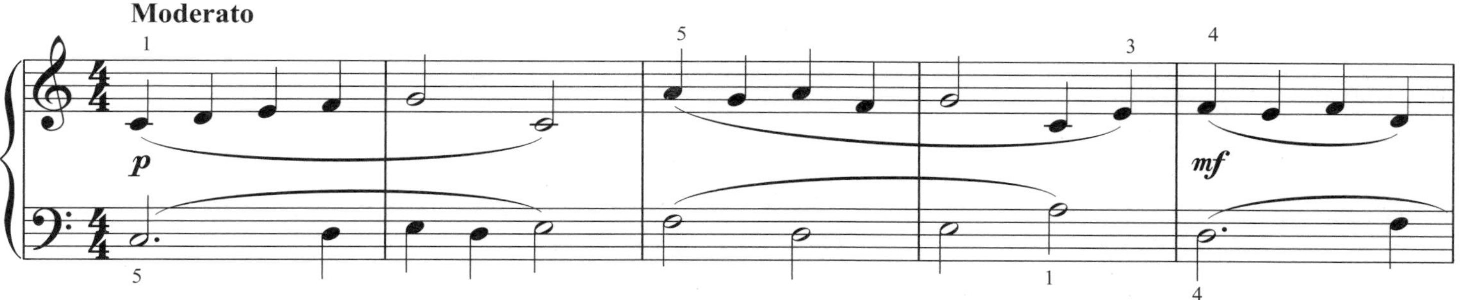

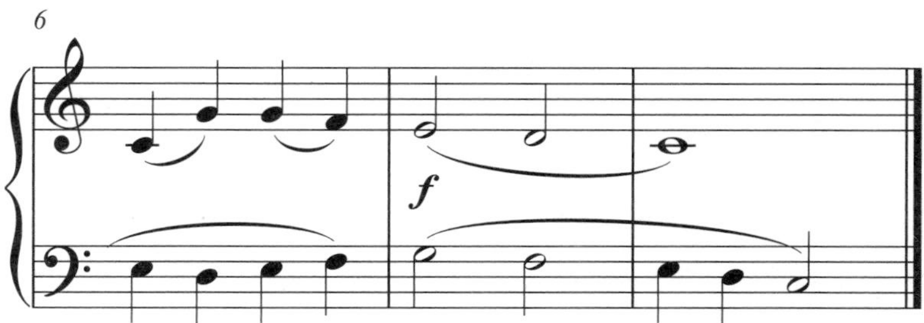

Exam advice

In an exam, you have half a minute to prepare your performance; use this time wisely.

- Check the key and time signature. You might want to remind yourself of the scale and arpeggio, checking for signs of major or minor first.
- Look for any accidentals, particularly when they apply to more than one note in the bar.
- Set the pace in your head and read through the piece, imagining the sound. It might help to sing part of the music or to clap or tap the rhythm. You can also try out any part of the test if you want to.
- Have you imagined the effect of the dynamics?

When the examiner asks you to play the piece, do not forget the pace you have set. Fluency is more important than anything else: make sure that you keep going whatever happens. If you make a little slip, do not go back and change it. Give a performance of the piece: if you can play the pieces in this book you will be well-prepared, so enjoy the opportunity to play another piece that you didn't know beforehand.

Sight reading requirements at a glance

The following table gives a general guide of the requirements pianists can expect to encounter at each level, and where they are encountered in this series of books. The complete detailed specifications can be found in the current syllabus. **Candidates should always refer to the requirements listed in the most recent syllabus when preparing for an exam.**

Sound at Sight 2nd Series	Grade	Keys*	Time signatures*	Note values*	Dynamics & tempi*	Articulation*
Book 1	Initial	C major	2/4	♩, 𝅗𝅥 and 𝄼	***p***, ***f*** and *moderato*	simple phrase marks
	Grade 1	G major; A minor (white notes only)	4/4	𝅝	***mf*** (maximum of 2 different dynamics)	
	Grade 2	A minor (including G sharp)	3/4	𝅗𝅥. and ties	*allegretto*	
Book 2	Grade 3	D minor		♫ and 𝄽	***mp*** and *andante*	slurs
	Grade 4	D major; E minor		♪, ♩. and 𝄾	< >	*staccato* & accents
Book 3	Grade 5	F, B♭, E♭ & A major; B & G minor (inc. modulation to dominant/relative major)	6/8	𝄽., ♪ and 𝅘𝅥𝅯	*rit.*, *rall.*, *accel.* and *a tempo*	pause; simple pedalling
	Grade 6	F♯ & C minor				pedalling required but not always marked
Book 4	Grade 7	E & A♭ major	9/8		any common terms	pedalling essential
	Grade 8	B & D♭ major; G♯ & B♭ minor (inc. double sharps & flats)	2/2 & changing time signatures	duplets/ triplets	*cresc.* and *dim.* as text ***ff***, ***pp*** change in terms; different dynamics for RH and LH	tenuto

*** Please note that at any given grade, candidates are also expected to know the requirements of the preceding grade(s).**